FOR RICHIEU

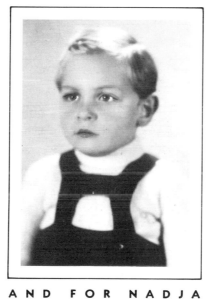

AND FOR NADJA

ART SPIEGELMAN, a cartoonist born after WW II, is working on a book about what happened to his parents as Jews in wartime Poland. He has made a series of visits to his childhood home in Rego Park, N.Y., to record his father's memories. Art's mother, Anja, committed suicide in 1968. Art becomes furious when he learns that his father, **VLADEK**, has burned Anja's wartime memoirs. Vladek is remarried to Mala, another survivor. She complains often of his stinginess and lack of concern for her. Vladek, a diabetic who has suffered two heart attacks, is in poor health.

In Poland, Vladek had been a small-time textile salesman. In 1937 he married Anja Zylberberg, the youngest daughter of a wealthy Sosnowiec hosiery family. They had a son, Richieu, who died during the war.

Forced first into ghettos, then into hiding, Vladek and Anja tried to escape to Hungary with their prewar acquaintances, the Mandelbaums, whose nephew, Abraham, had attested in a letter that the escape route was safe. They were caught and, in March, 1944, they were brought to the gates of Auschwitz.

PANTHEON BO

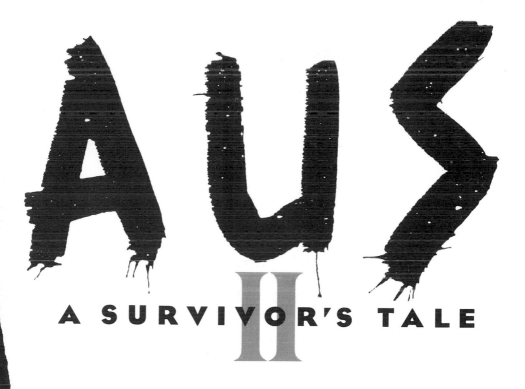

AUS

II A SURVIVOR'S TALE

AND HERE MY TROUBLES BEGAN

art spiegelman

OK   ORK

"Mickey Mouse is the most miserable ideal ever revealed....Healthy emotions tell every independent young man and every honorable youth that the dirty and filth-covered vermin, the greatest bacteria carrier in the animal kingdom, cannot be the ideal type of animal....Away with Jewish brutalization of the people! Down with Mickey Mouse! Wear the Swastika Cross!"
—newspaper article, Pomerania, Germany, mid-1930s

Thanks to Paul Pavel, Deborah Karl, and Mala Spiegelman for helping this volume into the world.

Thanks to the John Simon Guggenheim Memorial Foundation for a fellowship that allowed me to focus on completing *Maus*.

And my thanks, with love and admiration, to Françoise Mouly for her intelligence, integrity, editorial skills, and for her love.

All rights reserved under International and Pan-American Copyright Conventions. Published in the United States by Pantheon Books, a division of Random House, Inc., New York, and simultaneously in Canada by Random House of Canada Limited, Toronto.

Chapters one through four were originally published in somewhat different form in *Raw* magazine between 1986 and 1991.

Library of Congress Cataloging-in-Publication Data
Spiegelman, Art.
Maus: a survivor's tale, II: and here my troubles began/Art Spiegelman.
p.   cm.
ISBN 0-394-55655-0
1. Spiegelman, Vladek—Comic books, strips, etc.
2. Holocaust, Jewish (1939-1945)—Poland—Biography—Comic books, strips, etc.
3. Holocaust survivors—United States—Biography—Comic books, strips, etc.
4. Spiegelman, Art—Comic books, strips, etc.
5. Children of Holocaust survivors—United States—Biography—Comic books, strips, etc. I. Title.
D804.3.S66   1991
940.53'18'0207—dc20   91-52739

Book design: art spiegelman and Louise Fili

Manufactured in the United States of America

First Edition

AND HERE MY TROUBLES BEGAN

(FROM MAUSCHWITZ TO THE CATSKILLS AND BEYOND)

CONTENTS

HALT!

CHAPTER ONE

11

12

14

14

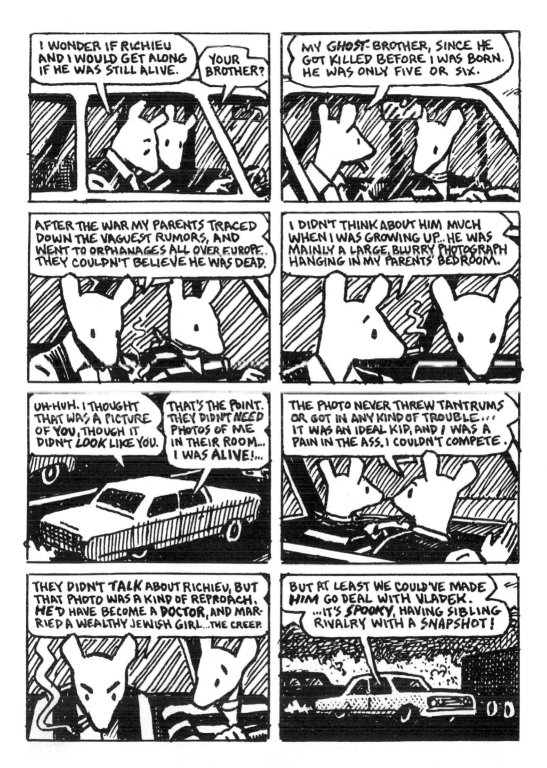

I NEVER FELT GUILTY ABOUT RICHIEU. BUT I DID HAVE NIGHTMARES ABOUT S.S. MEN COMING INTO MY CLASS AND DRAGGING ALL US JEWISH KIDS AWAY.

DON'T GET ME WRONG. I WASN'T OBSESSED WITH THIS STUFF ... IT'S JUST THAT SOMETIMES I'D FANTASIZE ZYKLON B COMING OUT OF OUR SHOWER INSTEAD OF WATER.

I KNOW THIS IS INSANE, BUT I SOMEHOW WISH I HAD BEEN IN AUSCHWITZ WITH MY PARENTS SO I COULD REALLY KNOW WHAT THEY LIVED THROUGH!

...I GUESS IT'S SOME KIND OF GUILT ABOUT HAVING HAD AN EASIER LIFE THAN THEY DID.

SIGH. I FEEL SO INADEQUATE TRYING TO RECONSTRUCT A REALITY THAT WAS WORSE THAN MY DARKEST DREAMS.

AND TRYING TO DO IT AS A COMIC STRIP! I GUESS I BIT OFF MORE THAN I CAN CHEW. MAYBE I OUGHT TO FORGET THE WHOLE THING.

THERE'S SO MUCH I'LL NEVER BE ABLE TO UNDERSTAND OR VISUALIZE. I MEAN, REALITY IS TOO COMPLEX FOR COMICS... SO MUCH HAS TO BE LEFT OUT OR DISTORTED.

JUST KEEP IT HONEST, HONEY.

SEE WHAT I MEAN... IN REAL LIFE YOU'D NEVER HAVE LET ME TALK THIS LONG WITHOUT INTERRUPTING.

HMMPH. LIGHT ME A CIGARETTE.

16

And so, the Catskills...

19

A few tense hours later...

ACCH, ARTIE. **AGAIN** YOU MADE THE WRONG ADDITION.

BUT LOOK- WE'VE CHECKED IT **TWICE**. IT'S **CORRECT**!

PFAH. IT DOESN'T COME OUT SO AS ON THE STATEMENT. WE'LL HAVE NOW EVERYTHING TO DO AGAIN.

WHA? THAT WOULD TAKE 2 OR 3 HOURS...IT'S OFF BY LESS THAN A BUCK. LET'S JUST FORGET IT.

ALWAYS YOU'RE SO **LAZY**! EVERY JOB WE SHOULD MAKE SO AS TO DO IT THE RIGHT WAY.

LAZY?! DAMN IT, YOU'RE DRIVING ME **NUTS**!

WAIT! WHY DON'T YOU TAKE A BREAK? I'LL FIND THE MISTAKE.

YES! WITH **FRANÇOISE** I CAN DO IT!

UM...I CAN HANDLE IT ALONE. WHY DON'T YOU **BOTH** GO OUT FOR A WALK?

THANKS A LOT.

WELL...DON'T MIX TOGETHER FOR ME ANY OF THE PAPERS. I'LL **REVIEW** WITH YOU WHEN I COME BACK...

...BUT FOR MY LEGS I COULD **USE** NOW THAT WE WALK A LITTLE.

SIGH. OKAY..I'LL GET MY TAPE RECORDER, SO TODAY ISN'T A **TOTAL LOSS**.

23

24

25

EVERYWHERE WE HAD TO RUN—SO LIKE JOGGERS—AND THEY RAN US TO THE SAUNA...

IT'S FREEZING!

JUST THANK GOD IT'S NOT GAS!

HERE IT WAS THE LIVE SHOWERS, NOT THE DEAD GAS SHOWERS WHAT WE HEARD SOMETIMES RUMORS.

IN THE SNOW THEY THREW TO US PRISONERS CLOTHINGS.

SCHNELL! SCHNELL! SCHNELL!

THEY NEVER EVEN LOOKED ON WHAT SIZE THEY THREW.

ONE GUY TRIED TO EXCHANGE.

E-EXCUSE ME. THESE SHOES ARE TOO SMALL.

MAYBE NOW THEY'LL FIT!

CRAK

THE SHOES WERE WOOD SHOES!

I WAS A LUCKY ONE. EVERYTHING FITTED ME A LITTLE. ONLY THE SHIRT WAS TORN AND TOO BIG FOR ME...

THEY REGISTERED US IN... THEY TOOK FROM US OUR NAMES. AND HERE THEY PUT ME MY NUMBER.

175113

26

ALL AROUND WAS A SMELL SO TERRIBLE, I CAN'T EXPLAIN... SWEETISH... SO LIKE RUBBER BURNING. AND *FAT*.

UNCLE! UNCLE!

WHEN WE CAME INSIDE THE GATES SOMEONE RAN TO US FROM FAR AWAY.

HERE WAS ABRAHAM— MANDELBAUM'S NEPHEW!

SO, UNCLE... YOU'VE ENDED UP HERE TOO.

YOU *TOLD* US TO COME!

YOU WROTE US ABOUT HOW *HAPPY* YOU ARE IN HUNGARY - THAT WE SHOULD JOIN YOU RIGHT AWAY! WELL ... HERE WE ARE.

HUN-GARY. HAH!

THE POLES WHO ARRANGED OUR "ESCAPE" UNDERSTOOD *YIDDISH*. SO THEY KNEW YOU WERE WAITING TO HEAR IF I WAS SAFE.

IN BIELSKO THE POLES DICTATED THAT LETTER WHILE THE GESTAPO HELD A PISTOL UP TO MY HEAD.

WHAT COULD I DO? THEY'D HAVE SHOT ME THEN AND THERE.

WELL... SO HERE'S OUR HUNGARY...

AND THERE'S ONLY ONE WAY OUT OF HERE FOR ALL OF US ... THROUGH THOSE CHIMNEYS.

ABRAHAM I DIDN'T SEE AGAIN.... I THINK HE CAME OUT THE CHIMNEY.

BUT I SAW AGAIN ONCE THE POLES WHO BETRAYED US.

THE GERMANS DIDN'T NEED THEM. SO THEY FINISHED ALSO IN AUSCHWITZ.

WE NEWCOMERS WERE PUT INSIDE A ROOM. OLD-TIMERS PASSED AND SAID ALL THE SAME.

YOU SEE THOSE CHIMNEYS?...

OKAY. SO I WAS MORE SAD.

I WAS WORN AND SHIVERING AND CRYING A LITTLE.

NOBODY EVEN LOOKED.

BUT FROM ANOTHER ROOM SOMEONE APPROACHED OVER

WHY ARE YOU CRYING, MY SON?

SHOULD I BE HAPPY? AM I AT A CARNIVAL?

LET ME SEE YOUR ARM...

HE WAS A PRIEST...

HMM... YOUR NUMBER STARTS WITH 17. IN HEBREW THAT'S "K'MINYAN TOV." SEVENTEEN IS A VERY GOOD OMEN...

HE WASN'T JEWISH - BUT VERY INTELLIGENT!

IT ENDS WITH 13, THE AGE A JEWISH BOY BECOMES A MAN...

AND LOOK! ADDED TOGETHER IT TOTALS 18. THAT'S "CHAI," THE HEBREW NUMBER OF LIFE.

I CAN'T KNOW IF I'LL SURVIVE THIS HELL, BUT I'M CERTAIN YOU'LL COME THROUGH ALL THIS ALIVE!

I STARTED TO BELIEVE. I TELL YOU, HE PUT ANOTHER LIFE IN ME.

AND WHENEVER IT WAS VERY BAD I LOOKED AND SAID: "YES. THE PRIEST WAS RIGHT! IT TOTALS EIGHTEEN.

WHEW, THAT GUY WAS A SAINT!

YES... I NEVER SAW HIM AGAIN.

28

FOR ME IT WAS HARD HERE, BUT FOR MY FRIEND MANDELBAUM IT WAS MORE HARD.

IN SOSNOWIEC, EVERYONE KNEW MANDELBAUM. HE WAS OLDER AS ME... NICE...A VERY RICH MAN...

...BUT NOW, IN AUSCHWITZ, MANDELBAUM WAS A MESS.

HIS PANTS WERE BIG LIKE FOR 2 PEOPLE, AND HE HAD NOT EVEN A PIECE OF STRING TO MAKE A BELT. HE HAD ALL DAY TO HOLD THEM WITH ONE HAND...

ONE SHOE. HIS FOOT WAS TOO BIG TO GO IN. THIS ALSO HE HAD TO HOLD SO HE COULD FIND MAYBE WITH WHOM TO EXCHANGE IT.

ONE SHOE WAS BIG LIKE A BOAT, BUT THIS AT LEAST HE COULD WEAR.

IT WAS WINTER, AND EVERYWHERE HE HAD TO GO AROUND WITH ONE FOOT ONTO THE SNOW.

CAN I USE YOUR SPOON, VLADEK?

OF COURSE, BUT WHERE'S YOURS?

I DROPPED IT, AND BY THE TIME I BENT DOWN, SOMEONE STOLE IT.

FOR A SPOON YOU COULD GET A HALF DAY'S BREAD.

I SPILLED MOST OF MY SOUP, TOO. WHEN I ASKED FOR MORE, THEY BEAT ME!

I HOLD ONTO MY BOWL AND MY SHOE FALLS DOWN. I PICK UP THE SHOE AND MY PANTS FALL DOWN...

BUT WHAT CAN I DO? I ONLY HAVE TWO HANDS!

MY GOD. PLEASE GOD... HELP ME FIND A PIECE OF STRING AND A SHOE THAT FITS!

BUT HERE GOD DIDN'T COME. WE WERE ALL ON OUR OWN.

IN THE MORNING, THE S.S. CHOSE WHO TO TAKE FOR THE DAY TO WORK. WEAK ONES THEY PUT ON THE SIDE TO TAKE AWAY FOREVER. BEFORE THEY CAME TO ME, THEY TOOK ENOUGH.

I KEPT CLOSE TO ME MANDELBAUM. AND WE WENT BACK SAFE INSIDE.

THE KAPO PUSHED THOSE REMAINING TO CLEAN UP IN THE BLOCK.

WAIT! SPIEGELMAN- YOU COME WITH ME!

EVERYONE THEY CALLED BY NUMBER BUT ME, HE CALLED BY NAME.

SIT HERE.... I'LL BE BACK SOON.

HERE I SAW ROLLS! I SAW EGGS! MEAT! COFFEE! ALL THE TABLE FULL! YOU KNOW WHAT IT WAS TO SEE SUCH THINGS?

IT MUST BE IT'S HIS BREAKFAST. SEE HOW HAPPY HE HAS IT HERE!

I WAS AFRAID TO LOOK. I WAS SO HUNGRY, I COULD GRAB ALL OF IT!

WHAT ARE YOU WAITING FOR? SIT DOWN AND EAT!

THIS FOOD, IT WAS FOR ME.

I ATE, ATE, ATE AS HE WATCHED. THEN I TAUGHT HIM A COUPLE HOURS AND WE SPOKE A LITTLE.

BUT WHY ARE YOU STUDYING ENGLISH?

I SPEAK GERMAN AS WELL AS POLISH—THAT'S WHY I'M A KAPO. OTHERWISE I'D BE A NOTHING LIKE YOU...
NOW THE ALLIES ARE BOMBING THE REICH. IF THEY WIN THIS WAR, IT WILL BE WORTH SOMETHING TO KNOW ENGLISH!

34

SO YOU DON'T KNOW WHAT HAPPENED TO MANDELBAUM?

HE GOT KILLED. OR HE DIED. I KNOW THEY **FINISHED** HIM.

MAYBE ON THE WALK TO WORK, A GUARD GRABBED HIS CAP AWAY.

GO GET YOUR CAP - QUICK!

SO WHAT COULD HE DO? HE RAN TO PICK IT UP. AND THE GUARD SHOT ON HIM FOR TRYING TO ESCAPE.

THE GUARD GOT A CONGRATULATIONS AND A FEW DAYS VACATION FOR STOPPING THE ESCAPE.

I DON'T **KNOW** IF THIS WAS HOW IT WAS WITH MANDELBAUM — ONLY THAT VERY OFTEN THEY DID SO...

THEY WANTED ONLY TO FINISH EVERYONE OUT. IT WAS VERY HARD WORK AND VERY LITTLE FOOD.

...MAYBE THEY KICKED AND HIT HIM IN HIS HEAD BECAUSE HE COULDN'T WORK FAST ENOUGH.

...OR MAYBE HE GOT SICK. SO THEY PUT HIM FIRST IN THE "HOSPITAL" AND THEN IN THE OVEN...

YOU SEE HOW THEY DID? AND I HAD IT STILL HAPPY THERE. FOR **ME** IT WAS NOT YET THE END.

NEWCOMERS WERE AFRAID FROM ME. I LOOKED LIKE A **BIG SHOT** AND THE KAPO KEPT ME CLOSE.

THEY'LL WANT 200 WORKERS TOMORROW. I'VE ONLY GOT 180 STILL **REGISTERED** HERE. ...YOU'D BETTER HIDE IN MY ROOM...

FOR OVER TWO MONTHS I STAYED HERE SAFE AND TAUGHT TO HIM ENGLISH.

OF THE GROUP WHEN I ARRIVED, ONLY I REMAINED...

VLADEK, WHAT WAS YOUR PROFESSION BEFORE YOU WERE BROUGHT HERE?

I WORKED IN A *LOT* OF DIFFERENT BUSINESSES. WHY?

I'VE KEPT YOU HERE IN THE "QUARANTINE BLOCK" AS LONG AS I CAN. YOU'LL HAVE TO BE ASSIGNED OUT TO A WORK CREW... SKILLED WORKERS GET BETTER TREATMENT.

I CAN DO *ANYTHING* ONCE I'M SHOWN HOW. IN THE GHETTO I WORKED IN A WOOD SHOP... IN SOSNOWIEC I WAS A TINSMITH.

A TIN-SMITH! I'LL SEE WHAT I CAN DO!

I WAS NOT *REALLY* A TINMAN. BUT I KNEW A LITTLE. IN SOSNOWIEC I WAS IN A TIN SHOP REGISTERED TO GET A SAFE WORK PASSPORT, AND I WATCHED HOW THEY WORKED.

ALWAYS AROUND AUSCHWITZ THEY WERE BUILD-ING. TO THE ROOFS THEY NEEDED GOOD TINMEN.

THE Pines GUESTS ONLY No Trespassing

UH-HUH. YOU TOLD ME. WHAT I WANTED TO ASK YOU ABOUT THOUGH, IS WHAT HAPPENED TO MOM WHILE YOU

STOP!...

Pi GUE No Tr

WE MUST TURN *QUICK* AND GO BY *THIS* ROAD TO COME TO THE PINES!

HUH?

ERVICE NTRANCE

IN THIS WAY THE HOTEL GUARD CAN'T SEE US, AND WE CAN SIT ON THEIR PATIO. IT'S *PRETTY* THERE TO SIT. I COME ALMOST EVERY DAY IN THIS WAY.

SOMETIMES I GET HERE FREE DANCING LESSONS, OR THEY HAVE FOR THE GUESTS FREE BINGO GAMES AND PRIZES.

36

AUSCHWITZ
(TIME FLIES)

Time flies...

42

43

And so...

EVERYBODY WAS SO HUNGRY ALWAYS, WE DIDN'T KNOW EVEN WHAT WE ARE DOING...

IN THE MORNING FOR BREAKFAST WE GOT ONLY A BITTER DRINK MADE FROM ROOTS.

I WOKE BEFORE EVERYBODY TO HAVE TIME TO THE TOILET AND FIND STILL SOME TEA LEFT.

ONE TIME A DAY THEY GAVE A SOUP FROM TURNIPS. TO STAND NEAR THE FIRST OF THE LINE WAS NO GOOD. YOU GOT ONLY WATER.

MIX IT! MIX IT!

NEAR THE END WAS BETTER — SOLID THINGS TO THE BOTTOM FLOATED.

BUT TOO FAR TO THE END IT WAS ALSO NO GOOD

..BECAUSE MANY TIMES IT COULD BE NO SOUP ANYMORE.

AND ONE TIME EACH DAY THEY GAVE TO US A SMALL BREAD, CRUNCHY LIKE GLASS.

THE FLOUR THEY MIXED WITH SAWDUST TOGETHER — WE GOT ONE LITTLE BRICK OF THIS WHAT HAD TO LAST THE FULL DAY.

MOST GOBBLED IT RIGHT AWAY, BUT ALWAYS I SAVED A HALF FOR LATER.

AND IN THE EVENING WE GOT A SPOILED CHEESE OR JAM. IF WE WERE LUCKY A COUPLE TIMES A WEEK WE GOT A SAUSAGE BIG LIKE TWO OF MY FINGERS. ONLY THIS MUCH WE GOT

IF YOU ATE HOW THEY GAVE YOU, IT WAS JUST ENOUGH TO DIE MORE SLOWLY.

50

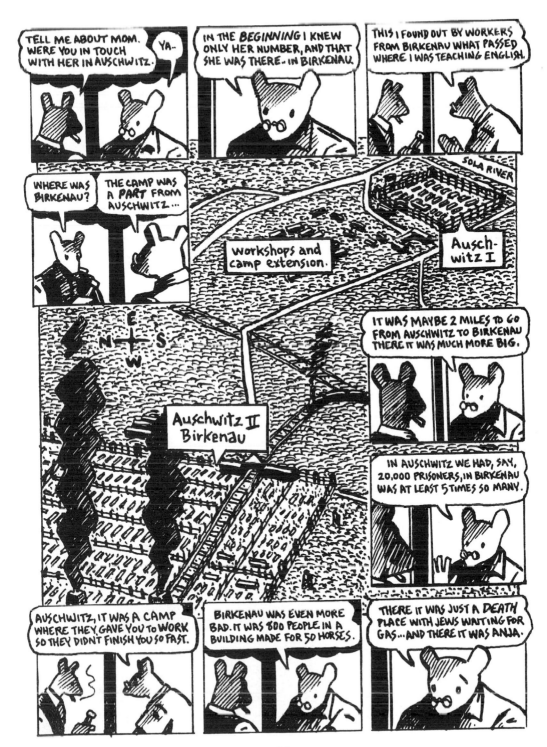

COME... IT'S TIME NOW WE'LL HURRY FOR LUNCH HOME TO THE BUNGALOW.

SO YOU WERE ACTUALLY IN *TOUCH* WITH ANJA IN BIRKENAU?

YAH. FROM MANCIE I HAD A REAL CONTACT WITH MOTHER, UNTIL LATER I COULD BRING ANJA TO—

WAIT! WHO'S MANCIE?

SHE WAS A HUNGARIAN, MANCIE, WHO WORKED SOMETIMES THERE. BEAUTIFUL. A TALL BLONDE GIRL. AND CLEVER.

REST BEHIND THAT STACK OF WOOD. I'LL WARN YOU IF A GUARD COMES CLOSE.

SHE HAD A LOVER, I HEARD LATER, AN S.S. MAN. HE GOT FOR HER A GOOD POSITION OVER 10 OR 12 OTHER GIRLS FROM BIRKENAU.

(PSST, MISS—UP HERE! I SEE HOW KIND YOU ARE. HELP ME. PLEASE!)

HUH? (WHAT DO YOU WANT?)

(NOTHING FOR ME, BUT I'M AFRAID FOR MY WIFE IN BIRKENAU. CAN YOU FIND OUT IF SHE'S STILL ALIVE?)

I TOLD TO HER ANJA'S NAME AND NUMBER.

(I'VE SAVED SOME FOOD. I CAN PAY FOR YOUR HELP.)

(KEEP YOUR FOOD. WE'LL BE WORKING HERE AGAIN IN A FEW DAYS. I'LL SEE WHAT I CAN FIND OUT.)

EACH DAY I LOOKED. FOUR DAYS AFTER, I SAW HER.

I MET A WOMAN NAMED ANJA FROM SOSNOWIEC. SHE'S VERY FRAIL...

SHE SPOKE OVER TO ONE OF HER WORKERS; I SPOKE ONLY TO MY TIN SO NOBODY WILL NOTICE.

SOMEONE TOLD HER THAT HER HUSBAND IS STILL ALIVE AND SHE STARTED SOBBING WITH JOY.

I HEARD THIS, AND I STARTED ALSO CRYING A LITTLE. AND MANCIE, SHE TOO STARTED CRYING.

A FEW DAYS AFTER, MANCIE AGAIN CAME THERE.

I PUT SOME "GARBAGE" UNDER A ROCK NEAR THE DOORWAY.

SHE BROUGHT TO ME A LETTER— A REAL LETTER!—FROM ANJA.

"I MISS YOU," SHE WROTE TO ME "EACH DAY I THINK TO RUN INTO THE ELECTRIC WIRES AND FINISH EVERYTHING, BUT TO KNOW YOU ARE ALIVE IT GIVES ME STILL TO HOPE..."

SHE TOLD ME HER KAPO WAS VERY MEAN ON HER AND GAVE WORK ANJA REALLY COULDN'T DO.

LIKE TO RUN FROM THE KITCH-EN WITH THE BIG CANS OF SOUP.

EVEN FOR ME SUCH CANS WERE HEAVY, AND FOR ANJA-SHE WAS SO SMALL-IT WAS IMPOSSIBLE.

SHE COULDN'T HOLD WELL HER END. ALWAYS SHE SPILLED.

THE KAPO BEAT ANJA VERY HARD BUT KEPT HER TO THIS JOB.

AND IF ANJA SPILLED OVER ALL FROM THE SOUP, THEN NOBODY GOT WHAT TO EAT, ESPECIALLY ANJA.

I WROTE TO HER, "I THINK OF YOU ALWAYS," AND SENT WITH MANCIE TWO PIECES OF BREAD.

IF THE S.S. WOULD SEE SHE IS TAKING FOOD INTO THE CAMP, RIGHT AWAY THEY WILL KILL HER.

BUT ALWAYS SHE TOOK.

SO SHE SAID, "IF A COUPLE IS LOVING EACH OTHER SO MUCH, I MUST HELP HOWEVER I CAN."

WHEN I VISITED TO ANJA THERE, I SAW WITH MY OWN EYES HOW IT WAS...

YOU SAW ANJA?

YA. EVERY FEW DAYS IT CAME AN S.S. COMMISSION TO THE TIN SHOP...

YOU HAVE MORE WORKERS THAN YOU NEED HERE...

GIVE US 10 PRISONERS TO TAKE BACK TO THE MAIN CAMP FOR OTHER WORK.

WELL...TAKE THAT ONE...AND THAT ONE—

AND—WAIT! DON'T TAKE HIM! HE'S ONE OF MY BEST ROOFERS... TAKE THAT ONE...AND THAT ONE—

THE UNLUCKY ONES WENT OVER FOR BAD JOBS, BUT ME YIDL KEPT PROTECTED.

...SEND A CREW TO SECTOR BIb IN BIRKENAU. SOME OF THE ROOFS IN THE WOMEN'S CAMP HAVE COLLAPSED.

LET ME GO TO BIRKENAU. I'VE NEVER SEEN IT.

GO, SPIEGELMAN, AND DON'T COME BACK FOR ALL I CARE. BAH! I GIVE UP MY BEST TINMEN, AND YOU I SAVE.

WHY?!

SO I MARCHED WITH A FEW TIN-MEN OVER TO BIRKENAU. I CAME THE FIRST TIME IN SUMMER 1944.

THOUSANDS—HUNDREDS OF THOUSANDS OF HUN-GARIANS WERE ARRIV-ING THERE AT THIS TIME.

I WAS A *FEW* TIMES IN BIRKENAU, AND ONCE I HAD *REALLY* TROUBLES. I WAS GOING FROM WORK AND PASSED BY ANJA...

VLADEK! VLADEK! VLADEK!

ANJA! DARLING! DID YOU GET THE FOOD I SENT YOU?

YES. YOU ALWAYS ARRANGE MIRACLES.

I THINK ABOUT YOU ...ALWAYS.

WE SPOKE A MINUTE ONLY AND I WENT ON MY WAY.

A GUARD SCREAMED TO ME:

HALT!

WHO WERE YOU TALKING TO?

N-NOBODY...

A STRANGER ASKED IF I KNEW HER BROTHERS IN AUSCHWITZ. I DIDN'T KNOW ANYTHING, SO I HARDLY ANSWERED.

GET INSIDE!

WHEN I'M FINISHED WITH YOU, YOU'LL KNOW *SOMETHING*, JEWISH PIMP! YOU'RE NOT HERE TO FLIRT AND GOSSIP.

COUNT THE BLOWS. IF YOU LOSE COUNT—I'LL START AGAIN!

EINS!
ZWEI!
DREI!

SO HE BEAT ME, WHAT CAN I TELL YOU? ONLY, THANK GOD, ANJA DIDN'T GET *ALSO* SUCH A BEATING. SHE WOULDN'T LIVE.

59

SO... IN THE TINSHOP I HAD STILL THE SAME STORY WITH YIDL.

ONLY ONE APPLE FOR ME TODAY? IS BUSINESS BAD, MR. CAPITALIST?

WHAT HAPPENED TO THE SHOEMAKER WHO WORKED IN THERE?

A LOT OF THE POLISH PRISONERS WERE SENT TO CAMPS INSIDE THE REICH. THEY TOOK SOME OF MY BOYS TOO.

I RAN TO THE KAPO IN CHARGE FROM ALL THE SHOP.

DO YOU NEED A NEW SHOEMAKER?

SURE. THE S.S. TOOK THE OLD ONE AWAY, BUT THEY'RE STILL BRINGING SHOES IN!

YOU KNOW, I'VE BEEN A SHOEMAKER SINCE CHILDHOOD.

YOU DON'T *LOOK* LIKE A SHOEMAKER TO ME ... YOU'RE A *TINMAN!*

DO I HAVE TO HAVE IT WRITTEN ON MY FOREHEAD?

ALRIGHT, THEN... FIX *THIS!*

I LEARNED A LITTLE SHOE FIXING WATCHING HOW THEY WORKED WHEN I WAS WITH MY COUSIN MILOCH, THERE IN THE GHETTO SHOE SHOP.

TO FIX SUCH AN OPENED SOLE I KNEW TO TAKE A DOUBLE THREAD SMEARED WITH WAX.

...MAKE THEN A HOLE AND PUSH THE THREAD HALF WAY ONLY.

AND ON THE UPPER PART PUT TWO HOLES EVEN TO THE SOLE...

BRING THE THREAD THEN THROUGH *THESE* HOLES.

CROSS THE THREAD FROM THE TOP AND BOTTOM, *BOTH* ENDS THROUGH A NEW HOLE IN THE SOLE AND REPEAT SO UNTIL THE SHOE IS CLOSED.

...AND SO IT'S MADE, YOU CAN'T EVEN *SEE* IT HAS STITCHES!

YOU'RE BETTER THAN OUR *LAST* SHOEMAKER!

YOU SEE? IT'S GOOD TO KNOW HOW TO DO *EVERYTHING!*

SO, NOW I WAS A SHOEMAKER. I HAD HERE A WARM AND PRIVATE ROOM WHERE TO SIT...

HA! I KNEW YOU WERE AN EXPERT TINMAN, BUT I NEVER KNEW YOU HAD SO MANY OTHER TALENTS!

AND HERE I DIDN'T HAVE ANYMORE TO WORRY WILL YIDL GIVE ME OUT.

OFFICIALS LIKED BETTER IF I FIX THEIR SHOES THAN TO SEND TO THE BIG SHOP INSIDE CAMP

THIS IS A NEW BOOT. I DON'T WANT YOUR REPAIR TO SHOW.

IT'S A BAD RIP... I'LL DO MY BEST.

IF IT DOESN'T LOOK BRAND NEW BY TOMORROW YOU WON'T BE HERE ANYMORE. UNDERSTAND ME?

I KNEW TO FIX SOLES AND HEELS, BUT WHAT THIS GESTAPO WANTED, IT NEEDED A SPECIALIST.

SO, GOING FROM WORK, I HID THIS BOOT TO SNEAK IT TO A REAL SHOEMAKER IN AUSCHWITZ.

CAN YOU FIX THIS? I'LL GIVE YOU A DAY'S RATION OF BREAD.

FOR A DAY'S RATION OF BREAD I CAN FIX ANYTHING!

I WATCHED CAREFUL HOW HE DID, SO NEXT TIME I CAN SAVE MYSELF SUCH A BREAD.

NEXT DAY I HAD THE BOOT READY FOR THIS GESTAPO.

HMM

HE LEFT THE BOOT AND WENT WITHOUT ONE WORD.

AND HE CAME BACK WITH A WHOLE SAUSAGE.

YOU DID A GOOD JOB.

YOU KNOW WHAT THIS WAS, A WHOLE SAUSAGE? YOU CAN'T IMAGINE! I CUT WITH A SHOE KNIFE AND ATE SO FAST I WAS A LITTLE SICK AFTER.

I COULDN'T ANYMORE MAKE A BUSINESS SMUGGLING WITH POLISH WORKERS FROM HERE AS A SHOEMAKER, BUT STILL I WAS WELL-OFF....

THE GESTAPO WHAT I FIXED HIS BOOT RECOMMENDED ME, SO HIS FRIENDS WANTED I'LL FIX ALSO THEIR SHOES AND PAID ME FOOD.

I SHARED SOMETIMES TO THE KAPO IN CHARGE.

I JUST ORGANIZED SOME EGGS—WANT ONE?

WHAT A FRIENDLY JEW! SURE—WE CAN COOK THEM ON MY HEATER.

IF YOU WANT TO LIVE, IT'S GOOD TO BE FRIENDLY.

AND HERE'S A LITTLE BREAD FOR OUR MEAL.

GREAT! SAY, WHAT ARE ALL THOSE NEW BUILDINGS THEY'RE PUTTING UP THERE?

JUST SOME NEW WORKSHOPS. THEY'RE EXPANDING THE UNION WERKE MUNITIONS FACTORY...

AND THEY'RE PUTTING UP SOME BARRACKS TO MOVE SOME WOMEN WORKERS FROM BIRKENAU OVER HERE.

M-MY WIFE IS IN BIRKENAU. MAYBE I COULD GET HER INTO ONE OF THOSE BARRACKS!

HAH! IMPOSSIBLE! IT WOULD COST A FORTUNE IN BRIBES!

HE UNWRAPPED SOME CHEESE AND ATE HIMSELF A PIECE.

PLEASE. COULD I HAVE THAT PIECE OF PAPER?

WELL, SURE. I CAN LET YOU HAVE THE PAPER— BUT NOT THE CHEESE!

I NEEDED TO WRITE OVER TO ANJA!

EVEN PAPER WAS HARD TO HAVE THERE. MY FRIENDS CAME ALWAYS TO ME WHEN THEY NEEDED.

I FOUND AND SAVED. FOR THE TOILET MOST USED A PIECE FROM THEIR CLOTHES OR THEIR HAND.

WHY DIDN'T OTHER PEOPLE SAVE PAPER?

ACH! YOU KNOW HOW MOST PEOPLE ARE!

SO... I WROTE OVER TO ANJA THAT NOW I AM A SHOEMAKER, AND I HEARD HERE ABOUT THESE NEW BARRACKS...

AND MANCIE TOOK IT, SHE WAS SO GOOD, ALWAYS SHE TOOK.

ON THE BACK FROM MY LETTER ANJA WROTE HOW MUCH SHE WANTED ONLY TO COME TO SUCH A BARRACK NEAR TO ME.

ANJA'S BARRACK WAS MAYBE 1000 GIRLS WITH A BAD KAPO WHAT HIT ANYBODY WHAT CAME NEAR.

SNEAK! I SAW YOU TAKE A SECOND PIECE OF BREAD!

NO.1—

SHE HAD LEATHER BOOTS—NOT WOOD. THEY WERE IN A VERY BAD SHAPE, BUT REALLY LEATHER.

N-NICE BOOTS—IT'S A PITY THE SOLES ARE COMING APART.

SO? WHAT DO YOU CARE?

YOU COULD SEND THEM TO MY HUSBAND HE'S A SHOEMAKER IN AUSCHWITZ....

OH, REALLY

SO, SHE ARRANGED THE BOOTS OVER TO ME.

OF COURSE I FIXED VERY NICE THE SHOES, AND THE KAPO THEN WAS VERY DIFFERENT WITH ANJA.

THAT SOUP CAN IS TOO HEAVY FOR YOU. COME REST IN MY ROOM UNTIL THE APPEL.

...VERY DIFFERENT.

I THOUGHT ONLY HOW HAPPY IT WOULD BE TO HAVE ANJA SO NEAR TO ME IN THESE NEW BARRACKS.

IT COULD BE "ARRANGED" FOR 100 CIGARETTES AND A BOTTLE VODKA, BUT THIS WAS A FORTUNE.

one day's bread. = 3 cigarettes

200 cigarettes = 1 bottle of vodka

HOW COULD YOU GET CIGARETTES?

EACH WEEK TO THE WORKERS, THEY GAVE US THREE.

THEY ISSUED A LUXURY LIKE THAT?

YA. AND IF YOU DON'T SMOKE YOU CAN EXCHANGE FOR BREAD.

I STARVED A LITTLE TO PAY TO BRING ANJA OVER.

ALL WHAT I ORGANIZED I KEPT IN A BOX UNDER MY MATTRESS.

BUT, WHEN I CAME BACK ONE TIME FROM WORK...

IT—IT'S GONE!

I'M TELLING YOU I WANTED TO CRY.

YOU LEFT THE BOX IN THE BARRACK? HOW COULD IT NOT BE TAKEN?

I DIDN'T THINK ON IT...

BUT EVERYONE WAS STARVING TO DEATH! SIGH-I GUESS I JUST DON'T UNDERSTAND.

YES...ABOUT AUSCHWITZ, NOBODY CAN UNDERSTAND.

SO... I SAVED A SECOND TIME A FORTUNE, AND GAVE OVER BRIBES TO BRING ANJA CLOSE TO ME. AND IN THE START OF OCTOBER, 1944, I SAW A FEW THOUSAND WOMEN IN THESE NEW BARRACKS...

AND WITH THEM WAS ANJA. THIS I ARRANGED. IT WAS THE ONLY TIME I WAS HAPPY IN AUSCHWITZ.

WHEN NOBODY SAW I WENT BACK AND FORTH UNTIL I SAW HER FROM FAR GOING TO MAKE MUNITIONS...

SHE WENT ALSO BACK AND FORTH UNTIL IT WAS SAFE TO APPROACH OVER TO MY FOOD PACKAGES...

BUT ONE TIME, IT WAS VERY BAD.

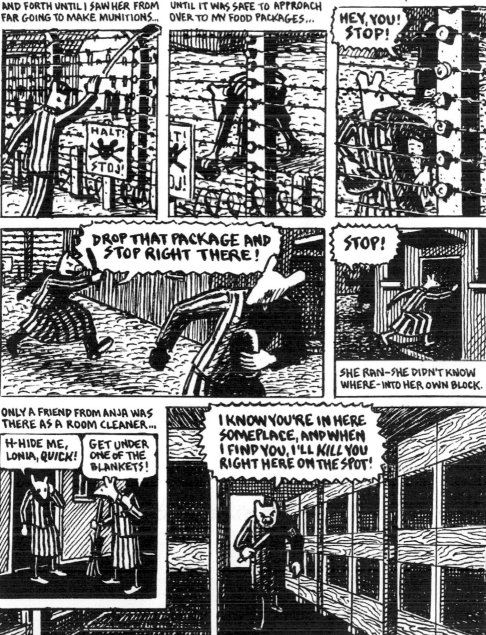

HEY, YOU! STOP!

DROP THAT PACKAGE AND STOP RIGHT THERE!

STOP!

SHE RAN—SHE DIDN'T KNOW WHERE—INTO HER OWN BLOCK.

ONLY A FRIEND FROM ANJA WAS THERE AS A ROOM CLEANER...

H-HIDE ME, LONIA, QUICK!

GET UNDER ONE OF THE BLANKETS!

I KNOW YOU'RE IN HERE SOMEPLACE, AND WHEN I FIND YOU, I'LL KILL YOU RIGHT HERE ON THE SPOT!

IT WAS SEVERAL ROOMS THERE, AND HUNDREDS OF BEDS. IN ONE, ANJA LAY SHAKING, AFRAID TO BREATHE EVEN.

65

I HAD TO STOP SENDING OVER SUCH PACKAGES MORE TO ANJA.

I LOST ANYWAY MY JOB NEAR TO HER SOON AFTER. MY WHOLE WORKSHOP THEY CLOSED OUT...

THEY PUT US BACK TO THE MAIN CAMP AND TOOK ME FOR *BLACK* WORK.

BLACK WORK?

CARRYING BACK AND FORTH BIG STONES, DIGGING OUT HOLES, EACH DAY DIFFERENT, BUT ALWAYS THE SAME. VERY HARD...

AND GOD FORBID, IF YOU STOPPED ONLY A MINUTE TO *BREATHE.*

YOU GOT A HIT TO THE HEAD, OR WORSE.

TO ME THEY NEVER HIT, BECAUSE I WORKED ALL MY MUSCLES AWAY.

I LIKED BETTER INDOORS WORK. I SOMETIMES WAS A "BETTNACH-ZIEHER"... A BED-AFTER-PULLER...

AFTER EVERYBODY FIXED THEIR BED, WE CAME TO FIX BETTER, SO THE STRAW LOOKED SQUARE.

WHAT A CRAZY JOB!

NO. THEY WANTED EVERYTHING NEAT AND IN GOOD ORDER.

BUT THESE DAYS I GOT TOO SKINNY AND IT CAME AGAIN A *SELEKTION.*

BLOCKSPERRE!

NOW IT COULD BE MY TURN.

RIGHT AWAY I RAN INSIDE THE TOILETS. AND IF SOMEBODY LOOKED, I'LL TELL I HAD A BAD STOMACH. WHAT HAD I TO LOSE?

NOBODY LOOKED, SO I SAT LUCKY THE WHOLE SELEKTION.

I CAME TO ONE OF THE FOUR CREMO BUILDINGS. IT LOOKED SO LIKE A BIG BAKERY...

FROM BELOW GROUND, IN THE GAS ROOM, WE TINMEN HAD TO TAKE OUT THE PIPES AND FANS FOR VENTILATING.

THIS WAS A FACTORY TO MAKE —ONE, TWO, THREE— ASHES AND SMOKE FROM ALL WHAT CAME HERE.

underground undressing room

ovens

underground gas chamber

EXE-CUTION ROOM

UNDRESS-ING ROOM

RM. FOR MELTING GOLD FILLINGS

CORPSE LIFT

GAS CHAMBER

INCINERATION ROOM OVENS

CHIMNEY

COAL STORAGE

TOILET

CREMATORIUM II.

SPECIAL PRISONERS WORKED HERE SEPARATE. THEY GOT BETTER BREAD, BUT EACH FEW MONTHS THEY ALSO WERE SENT UP THE CHIMNEY. ONE FROM THEM SHOWED ME EVERYTHING HOW IT WAS.

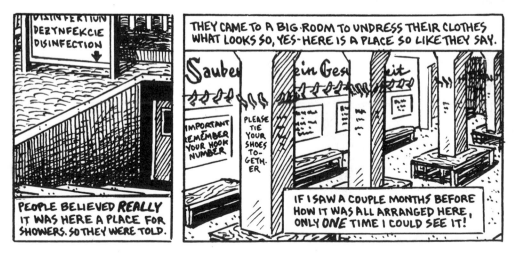

DISINFEKTION
DEZYNFEKCIE
DISINFECTION

PEOPLE BELIEVED REALLY IT WAS HERE A PLACE FOR SHOWERS. SO THEY WERE TOLD.

THEY CAME TO A BIG ROOM TO UNDRESS THEIR CLOTHES WHAT LOOKS SO, YES-HERE IS A PLACE SO LIKE THEY SAY.

Sauber ein Gesundheit

IMPORTANT REMEMBER YOUR HOOK NUMBER

PLEASE TIE YOUR SHOES TO-GETH-ER

IF I SAW A COUPLE MONTHS BEFORE HOW IT WAS ALL ARRANGED HERE, ONLY ONE TIME I COULD SEE IT!

AND EVERYBODY CROWDED INSIDE INTO THE SHOWER ROOM, THE DOOR CLOSED HERMETIC, AND THE LIGHTS TURNED DARK.

Zyklon B, a pesticide, dropped into hollow columns.

IT WAS BETWEEN 3 AND 30 MINUTES— IT DEPENDED HOW MUCH GAS THEY PUT— BUT SOON WAS NOBODY ANYMORE ALIVE.

THE BIGGEST PILE OF BODIES LAY RIGHT NEXT TO THE DOOR WHERE THEY TRIED TO GET OUT.

THIS GUY WHO WORKED THERE, HE TOLD ME...

WE PULLED THE BODIES APART WITH HOOKS. BIG PILES, WITH THE STRONGEST ON TOP, OLDER ONES AND BABIES CRUSHED BELOW... OFTEN THE SKULLS WERE SMASHED ...

THEIR FINGERS WERE BROKEN FROM TRYING TO CLIMB UP THE WALLS,...AND SOMETIMES THEIR ARMS WERE AS LONG AS THEIR BODIES, PULLED FROM THE SOCKETS.

ENOUGH!

I DIDN'T WANT MORE TO HEAR, BUT ANYWAY HE TOLD ME.

THEY PULLED THE BODIES WITH AN ELEVATOR UP TO THE OVENS— MANY OVENS — AND TO EACH ONE THEY BURNED 2 OR 3 AT A TIME.

TO SUCH A PLACE FINISHED MY FATHER, MY SISTERS, MY BROTHERS, SO MANY

71

WHAT ARE THEY DOING OVER THERE - DIGGING TRENCHES IN CASE THE RUSSIANS ATTACK?

TRENCHES...HAH! THOSE ARE GIANT *GRAVES* THEY'RE FILLING IN!...

IT STARTED IN MAY AND WENT ON ALL SUMMER. THEY BROUGHT JEWS FROM HUNGARY - TOO MANY FOR THEIR OVENS, SO THEY DUG THOSE BIG CREMATION PITS.

THE HOLES WERE BIG, SO LIKE THE SWIMMING POOL OF THE PINES HOTEL HERE.

AND TRAIN AFTER TRAIN OF HUNGARIANS CAME.

AND THOSE WHAT FINISHED IN THE GAS CHAMBERS BEFORE THEY GOT PUSHED IN THESE GRAVES, IT WAS THE *LUCKY* ONES.

THE OTHERS HAD TO JUMP IN THE GRAVES WHILE STILL THEY WERE ALIVE...

PRISONERS WHAT WORKED THERE POURED GASOLINE OVER THE LIVE ONES AND THE DEAD ONES.

AND THE FAT FROM THE BURNING BODIES THEY SCOOPED AND POURED AGAIN SO EVERYONE COULD BURN BETTER.

That night...

78

And so...

WE DIDN'T STAND ON THE LAST APPELS, BUT CAME UP TO THIS ATTIC.

SCREAMING GESTAPO CHASED EVERYWHERE. EACH PRISONER GOT A BREAD, A SAUSAGE AND A KICK OUT, OUT THE GATE, TO MARCH.

THEN THIS GUY FROM THE OFFICE RAN IN...

TERRIBLE NEWS! WE HAVE TO LEAVE!

THEY'RE GOING TO SET FIRE TO THE CAMP AND BOMB ALL THE BLOCKS! HURRY!

FINALLY THEY *DIDN'T* BOMB, BUT THIS WE COULDN'T KNOW. WE LEFT BEHIND EVERY-THING, WE WERE SO AFRAID, EVEN THE CIVILIAN CLOTHES WE ORGANIZED. AND RAN OUT!

IT WAS ALREADY NIGHT. THEY GAVE TO EACH OF US A BLANKET AND A LITTLE BIT FOOD TO CARRY, AND WE WENT OUT FROM AUSCHWITZ, MAYBE THE LAST ONE.

ALL NIGHT I HEARD SHOOTING. HE WHO GOT TIRED, WHO CAN'T WALK SO FAST, THEY SHOT.

THE MORE WE WALKED, THE MORE I HEARD SHOOTING...

AND IN THE DAYLIGHT, FAR AHEAD, I SAW IT.

SOMEBODY IS JUMPING, TURNING, ROLLING 25 OR 35 TIMES AROUND. AND STOPS.

"OH," I SAID. "THEY MAYBE KILLED THERE A DOG."

WHEN I WAS A BOY OUR NEIGHBOR HAD A DOG WHAT GOT MAD AND WAS BITING.

KPOW

THE NEIGHBOR CAME OUT WITH A RIFLE AND SHOT.

THE DOG WAS ROLLING SO, AROUND AND AROUND, KICKING, BEFORE HE LAY QUIET.

AND NOW I THOUGHT: "HOW AMAZING IT IS THAT A HUMAN BEING REACTS THE SAME LIKE THIS NEIGHBOR'S DOG."

ONE OF THE BOYS WHAT WE WERE IN THE ATTIC TOGETHER, TALKED OVER TO THE GUARD...

PSST_ LOOK. THE WAR IS ALMOST OVER. SOME OF US WANT TO ESCAPE INTO THE WOODS. WE CAN PAY...

?

SHARE THIS GOLD WITH THE GUARDS IN FRONT AND BEHIND. JUST DON'T SHOOT WHEN WE RUN...

WE'LL GIVE YOU THE SIGNAL LATE TO-NIGHT, AND SHOOT OVER YOUR HEADS.

ALL DAY LONG THEY WERE ARRANGING...

IT'S ALL SET, VLADEK. HELP PAY OFF THE GUARDS AND JOIN US.

ACH. HOW CAN YOU TRUST THE GERMANS?!

AT NIGHT WAS A COMMOTION. 8 OR 9 RAN OFF...

BANG

AND OF COURSE YOU COULDN'T TRUST...

SO THE MARCH WAS GOING AND GOING. FOREVER WE MARCHED. AND THE ONES WHAT DIDN'T FALL DOWN, WE MARCHED.

AND SO WE CAME OVER TO GROSS-ROSEN.

HERE WAS A SMALL CAMP, WITH NO GAS.

POLAND 1 INCH = 90 MILES
Breslau
GROSS-ROSEN
GERMANY
SUDETEN-LAND
CZECHOSLOVAKIA
Czestochowa
Krakow
AUSCH-WITZ

IT WAS THOUSANDS OF PRISONERS FROM ALL AROUND BEING PULLED BACK INTO GERMANY.

EVERYWHERE WAS CONFUSION AND HITTING. TERRIBLE!

YOU SHITS OVER THERE! GO HAUL THE SOUP FROM THE KITCHEN—TWO TO EACH PAIL.

THEY CAUGHT 20 OF US TO CARRY.

YOU SEE WHAT'S GOING ON HERE. STAY WITH ME!

I GRABBED FAST A GUY WHAT WAS STILL STRONG LIKE ME.

MOST COULDN'T EVEN LIFT THEY WERE WEAK FROM MARCHING AND NO FOOD.

QUICK! QUICK!

BEHIND I HEARD YELLING AND SHOUTING. I DIDN'T LOOK.

LAZY BASTARDS! LOOK AT HOW THOSE TWO RUN!

WE GOT AN EXTRA PORTION SOUP FOR THIS. MOST WERE NOT LUCKY TO BE STILL STRONG.

IN THE MORNING THEY CHASED US TO MARCH AGAIN OUT, WHO KNOWS WHERE...

THROUGH THE TOWN WE WERE GOING. IT WAS EMPTY, WITH NO PRIVATE PEOPLE. AND WE SAW, FROM FAR, A TRAIN.

IT WAS SUCH A TRAIN FOR HORSES, FOR COWS.

INSIDE! MOVE! MOVE!

THEY PUSHED UNTIL IT WAS NO ROOM LEFT.

WE LAY ONE ON TOP THE OTHER, LIKE MATCHES, LIKE HERRINGS.

I PUSHED TO A CORNER NOT TO GET CRUSHED...

HIGH UP I SAW A FEW HOOKS TO CHAIN UP MAYBE THE ANIMALS.

I HAD STILL THE THIN BLANKET THEY GAVE ME.

I CLIMBED TO SOMEBODY'S SHOULDER AND HOOKED IT STRONG.

IN THIS WAY I CAN REST AND BREATHE A LITTLE.

THIS SAVED ME. MAYBE 25 PEOPLE CAME OUT FROM THIS CAR OF 200.

85

THE TRAIN STAYED SO, WITHOUT MOVING, I DON'T KNOW HOW LONG, UP TO A WEEK...

THEN, ONE DAY THEY OPENED...

THROW OUT THE DEAD, AND CLEAN UP YOUR FILTH!

IF THE DEAD HAD BREAD LEFT, OR BETTER SHOES, WE KEPT...

OUTSIDE WERE MANY TRAINS STANDING FOR WEEKS, WHAT THEY *NEVER* OPENED, AND IT WAS EVERYONE DEAD INSIDE...

...THEY DIDN'T NEED ANYMORE.

THEY CLOSED US AGAIN. WE WERE VERY HAPPY WE HAD NOW ROOM WHERE TO STAND.

NEAR TO THE DOOR WE PILED NEW DEAD ONES. EACH DAY THE GERMANS OPENED: "HOW MANY DEAD?" AND WE THREW OUT, AND SOON WE HAD ROOM EVEN TO SIT.

THIS WAS EARLY FEBRUARY, IN 1945. IT WAS NO FOOD AND SO CROWDED—

LOOK WHERE YOU GO!

ACH! THE SHOP-RITE IS *THERE*, AND YOU DIDN'T TURN TO IT!

≈WHOOSH≈

SO, COME. WE'LL GO NOW IN TO GIVE BACK OUR GROCERIES.

NO WAY! I'M NOT GOING IN TO RETURN A LOAD OF OPEN BOXES AND PARTIALLY EATEN FOOD.

WHAT'S TO BE SO ASHAMED? IT'S FOODS I CAN'T EAT. YOU WAIT THEN IN THE CAR WHILE *I* ARRANGE IT.

Y'KNOW... I'LL BET YOU THAT ANJA'S NOTEBOOKS WERE WRITTEN ON BOTH SIDES OF THE PAGE...

HUH? I CAN'T REMEMBER. WHY D'YOU SAY THAT?

WELL... IF THERE WERE ANY *BLANK* PAGES VLADEK WOULD NEVER HAVE BURNED THEM.

UH HUH... HEY! YOU CAN SEE HIM IN THE WINDOW!

JEEZ. VLADEK AND THE MANAGER ARE SHOUTING AT EACH OTHER...

NOW THE MANAGER IS JUST WALKING AWAY FROM HIM...

AND NOW VLADEK IS TRAILING AFTER HIM...

HOW EMBARRASSING.

NOW WE'LL DRIVE BACK SO I CAN PHONE TO MY LAWYER ON MALA.

DACHAU...YOU WERE SAYING IT WAS VERY CROWDED IN THAT CAMP...

YAH-THIS WAS A CAMP—TERRIBLE! I HAD A MISERY, I CAN'T TELL YOU... HERE, IN DACHAU, MY TROUBLES BEGAN.

WE WERE CLOSED IN BARRACKS, SITTING ON STRAW, WAITING ONLY TO DIE.

IN THE STRAW, IT WAS LICE...

FROM THE LICE WAS TYPHUS.

TO EAT WE GOT ONLY BREAD AND SOUP, BUT YOU HAD TO SHOW FIRST YOUR SHIRT...

IF IT WAS ANY LICE, YOU GOT NO SOUP. THIS WAS IMPOSSIBLE. EVERYWHERE WAS LICE!

AND, GOD FORBID, IF SOMEONE GOT SOUP AND SOMEONE SPILLED HIM A DROP...

LIKE WILD ANIMALS THEY WOULD FIGHT UNTIL THERE WAS BLOOD.

YOU CAN'T KNOW WHAT IT IS, TO BE HUNGRY.

92

FROM THE INFIRMARY I HAD TO GO BACK TO A BAD BARRACK, WHERE WE WERE ALL DAY STANDING OUTSIDE.

PARLEZ-VOUS FRANÇAIS?

WHA? NO...

IT WAS NOTHING TO EAT, AND NOTHING TO DO, ONLY TO WAIT AND TO DIE.

I CAN SPEAK GERMAN, YIDDISH, POLISH AND ENGLISH.

ANGLAIS?!

DIEU MERCI! I TALK ENGLISH ALSO A LITTLE. I WAS BECOMING CRAZY!...

THERE IS NO OTHER FRENCH HERE AND I DO NOT KNOW TO TALK GERMAN. I HAD NOBODY TO WHO TO TALK.

YOU ARE A POLE-JEW, YES? HOW YOU KNOW ENGLISH?

ACCH... I DREAMED ALWAYS TO GO ONE DAY TO AMERICA...

SO, WE TALKED, AND IT MADE THE TIME LIGHTER.

EACH DAY HE FOUND ME, THE FRENCH MAN...

BRR. GOOD MORNING. IT IS AGAIN VERY COLD TODAY.

LOOK TO THIS, MY FRIEND. I HAVE A BOX!

HE WAS NOT A JEW, SO BY THE RED CROSS THEY LET PACKAGES COME TO HIM.

MY FAMILY SENDS. I WANT THAT YOU ALSO EAT SOMETHING.

MY GOD. SARDINES! BISCUITS! CHOCOLATE!

HE INSISTED TO SHARE WITH ME, AND IT SAVED ME MY LIFE.

93

WITH MY NEW FOOD I CAME TO AN IDEA...

PSST— DO YOU WANT TO BUY A BAR OF CHOCOLATE?

CHOCOLATE?! DO I LOOK LIKE A MILLIONAIRE?

I'LL TRADE IT FOR YOUR SHIRT.

MY SHIRT?! YOU'RE CRAZY—I'D FREEZE!

UM— GIVE ME YOUR DAY'S RATION OF BREAD TOO.

IN AUSCHWITZ A SHIRT WAS NOT SO EXPENSIVE, BUT HERE NO GOODS CAME IN.

I CLEANED THE SHIRT VERY, VERY CAREFUL.

AND OUTSIDE, I DRIED IT.

I WAS LUCKY TO FIND A PIECE OF PAPER...

SO, CAREFUL I WRAPPED IT.

I UNWRAPPED ONLY WHEN THEY CALLED TO SOUP...

HERE WAS A SHIRT WITH REALLY NO LICE!

MY OLD SHIRT I HID TO MY PANTS. I SHOWED THE NEW ONE.

OKAY.

RIGHT AWAY THEY GAVE ME TO EAT.

YOU ARE A GENIUS, VLADEK. A GENIUS!

I HELPED THE FRENCHMAN TO ALSO ORGANIZE A SHIRT. SO WE BOTH GOT ALWAYS SOUP.

94

BUT AFTER A FEW WEEKS I GOT TOO SICK EVEN TO EAT...

TYPHUS!

I GOT VERY HOT FEVER AND I COULDN'T SLEEP. *TYPHUS!*

EVERY NIGHT PEOPLE DIED OF THIS.

AT NIGHT I HAD TO GO TO THE TOILET DOWN. IT WAS ALWAYS FULL, THE WHOLE CORRIDOR, WITH THE DEAD PEOPLE PILED THERE. YOU COULDN'T GO THROUGH...

YOU HAD TO GO ON THEIR HEADS, AND THIS WAS TERRIBLE, BECAUSE IT WAS SO SLIPPERY, THE SKIN, YOU THOUGHT YOU ARE FALLING. AND THIS WAS EVERY NIGHT.

SO NOW I HAD TYPHUS, AND I HAD TO GO TO THE TOILET DOWN, AND I SAID, "NOW IT'S *MY* TIME. NOW I WILL BE LAYING LIKE THIS ONES AND SOMEBODY WILL STEP ON ME!"

I WAS ALIVE STILL THE NEXT TIME IT CAME A GUY FROM THE INFIRMARY...

MANY DIDN'T LIVE LONG ENOUGH TO GO TO DIE IN THE INFIRMARY.

THERE I LAY TOO WEAK EVEN TO MOVE OR TO GO TO THE TOILET OUT FROM BED.

I ASKED HELP FROM THE FELLOWS NEXT TO ME, BUT IN A FEW HOURS THEY WERE DEAD AND OTHERS CAME.

THEY GAVE BREAD AND SOUP, BUT I WAS TOO WEAK TO EAT...

SO I PUT MY PORTION BELOW MY PILLOW.

HEY! THERE'S STALE BREAD ALL OVER THIS ONE'S BED!

WELL, TAKE IT AWAY... HE'LL NEVER NEED IT.

I SCREAMED. BUT I **COULDN'T** SCREAM.

MMUH MMNH.

I WAS TOO WEAK TO SCREAM...

SO I TOOK MY SHOE AND KNOCKED LOUD.

KLAKK KLAKK KLAKK

STOP THAT RACKET!

BAH! KEEP YOUR DAMN BREAD!

I COULDN'T EAT, BUT I CUT PIECES TO PAY FOR HELP TO GO DOWN TO THE TOILET.

I ONLY DON'T KNOW HOW TO ARRANGE MYSELF... MAYBE TO YOUR ROOM I CAN FIND A TENANT TO TAKE CARE ON ME.

UH-HUH. MAY-BE...

WELL... COME! WE HAVE NOW TO CARRY UP MY STORM WINDOWS TO PUT IN.

SHIT. I WAS HOPING YOU'D TELL ME MORE OF YOUR STORY...

THIS WE CAN TALK MAYBE AFTER, BUT ALREADY I'M COLD. I LOSE MONEY TO HEAT WITH NO STORM WINDOWS.

SIGH.

IN OTHER YEARS I PUT BY NOW THE WINDOWS, THAT I DIDN'T NEED HELP.

LOOK... I'LL DO IT, BUT FIRST, JUST TELL ME MORE ABOUT ANJA.

ANJA? WHAT IS TO TELL? EVERYWHERE I LOOK I'M SEEING ANJA...

FROM MY GOOD EYE, FROM MY GLASS EYE, IF THEY'RE OPEN OR THEY'RE CLOSED, ALWAYS I'M THINKING ON ANJA.

UH, I MEANT WHEN YOU WERE IN DACHAU. WHERE WAS ANJA?

CLIK

I DON'T KNOW—TO DIFFERENT CAMPS... SHE MARCHED FROM AUSCHWITZ EARLIER AS ME, AND CAME ALSO THROUGH GROSS-ROSEN, AND THEN—I DON'T REMEMBER—

103

BUT HOW DID ANJA *SURVIVE*?

MANCIE—THE HUNGARIAN GIRL WHAT I KNEW THERE IN AUSCHWITZ—SHE KEPT ANJA CLOSE BY TO HER.

AFTER THE WAR I LOOKED ALWAYS FOR MANCIE, TO GIVE A NICE REWARD, BUT I DIDN'T KNOW EVEN HER FULL NAME, AND I NEVER FOUND!

MOM USED TO MENTION *RAVENSBRÜCK.* WAS MANCIE WITH HER THERE?

YAH... MAYBE IT WAS THERE...

I KNOW ONLY THAT ANJA CAME OUT FREE BY THE RUSSIAN SIDE AND SHE CAME BACK TO SOSNOWIEC BEFORE ME. MY LIBERATION, IT TOOK LONGER...

IT WAS THE LAST MINUTES OF THE WAR, I LEFT DACHAU...

I WENT TO BE EXCHANGED FOR GERMAN PRISONERS ON THE SWISS BORDER BUT WE NEVER CAME.

I REMEMBER WE GOT EACH A TREASURE BOX FROM THE SWISS RED CROSS: SARDINES! BISCUITS! CHOCOLATE!

SOME ATE RIGHT AWAY EVERYTHING. I KEPT, OF COURSE, TO HAVE LATER.

SO, AT NIGHT, SOME TRIED TO STEAL FROM ME...

HEY!

WITH MY TYPHUS I NEEDED STILL MUCH TO REST, BUT THIS TREASURE WAS MORE TO ME THAN SLEEPING.

104

111

I TOLD EVERYTHING HOW WE SURVIVED TO HERE...

...AND FROM DACHAU WE CAME OVER BY TRAIN TO— BANG BANG! All!

THAT'S JUST MY MEN SIGNALING THAT THEY FOUND A CACHE OF GERMAN AMMO...

THOSE KRAUTS CAN'T HURT YOU ANYMORE. THE ONLY ONES LEFT ARE DEAD OR DYING.

THIS HOUSE WILL BE PART OF OUR BASE CAMP...

BUT I GUESS YOU BOYS CAN STAY IF YOU KEEP THE JOINT CLEAN AND MAKE OUR BEDS.

WANT SOME CHOCO- LATE?

M-MAYBE FOR LATER. THANK YOU.

SO WE WORKED FOR THE AMERICANS AND THEY LIKED ME THAT I CAN SPEAK ENGLISH.

THANKS FOR THE SHINE, WILLIE.

IT'S OKAY, SERGEANT. DON'T EVEN MENTION.

THEY GAVE TO US FOOD CANS AND GIFTS AND CALLED TO ME "WILLIE."

112

114

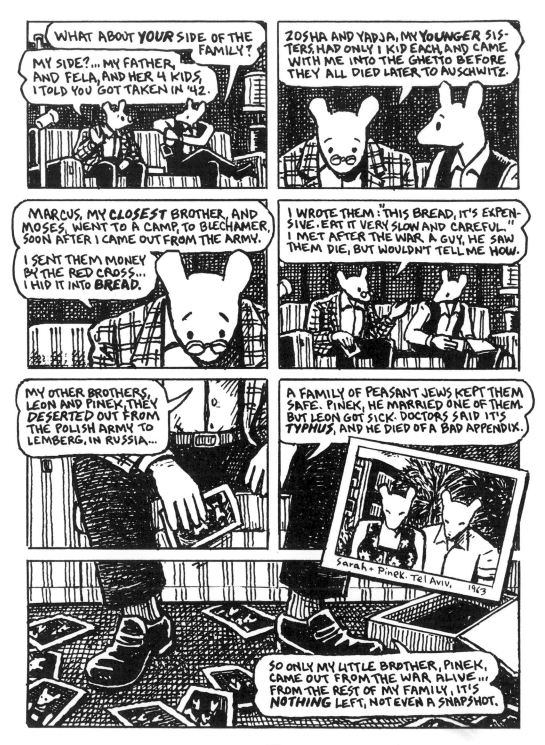

The SECOND HONEYMOON

Winter...

FLORIDA

HEY! EVERYTHING'S AL-MOST *PACKED,* MALA. THE MAIN REASON I FLEW DOWN WAS TO *HELP!*

PSSH. YOU KNOW VLADEK. WILD HORSES CAN'T HOLD HIM STILL... SO NOW HE'S EXHAUSTED, AND ME TOO.

GROAN

HI, POP. HOW ARE YOU?

TERRIBLE. SO WEAK... SO WEAK...

DID YOU ARRANGE EMERGENCY OXY-GEN FOR HIM ON TOMORROW'S PLANE?

UH-HUH. AND I'VE GOT AN AMBULANCE TO TAKE HIM AND ME FROM J.F.K. TO LAGUARDIA HOSPITAL. I'LL CHECK HIM IN WHILE FRANÇOISE DRIVES YOU HOME.

HOW DID YOU TWO GET BACK TOGETHER?

I DON'T KNOW. I GOT A CALL FROM THE HOSPI-TAL AND FELT SORRY FOR HIM. I WENT OVER.

I *SWORE* I'D NEVER SEE HIM AGAIN, BUT I'M JUST A SUCKER. HE TALKED UNTIL I WAS BLUE IN THE FACE... AND HERE I AM.

MALA, MALA! COME QUICK!

ANJA MUST HAVE BEEN A *SAINT!* NO WONDER SHE KILLED HERSELF.

HE'S CALL-ING YOU.

IT'S JUST HIS *STOOL.* HE WANTS ME TO CHECK IT BEFORE HE'LL FLUSH. HE'S AS DIFFICULT AS EVER.

BUT NOW HE'S MORE CON-FUSED AND DEPENDENT. ...WHAT CAN I DO? HE *TRAPPED* ME.

Next morning...

IN THE U.S., UNCLE HERMAN AGAIN HAD A HOSIERY FACTORY. BY HIM I GOT FULL-LENGTH NYLON STOCKINGS.

THESE IT WAS IMPOSSIBLE TO FIND IN SWEDEN.

YOU WANT MY NYLONS TO BUY?

DO I?! MY CUSTOMERS WILL KILL FOR THESE. THEY'RE RATIONED!

HOW MUCH?

NORMAL PRICE. BUT TO EACH PAIR YOU MUST TAKE ALSO A PAIR OF MY KNEE-LENGTHS.

I'LL THROW THEM AWAY, BUT IT'S WORTH IT!

AND I SOLD OUT THE WHOLE INVENTORY.

I BECAME SO, LIKE A PARTNER TO THIS DEPARTMENT STORE AND VERY WELL-OFF.

WHEN IT CAME A FEW YEARS LATER OUR VISAS TO AMERICA, THE STORE MADE A BIG SURPRISE PARTY.

YOU CAN STILL RIP UP YOUR BOAT TICKETS AND STAY!

BON VOYAGE

REALLY I WAS SORRY TO GO.

I MADE IN THE STATES A LIVING DEALING DIAMONDS, BUT NEVER I HAD IT AGAIN SO GOOD.

SIGH. COME, WE'LL GO NOW INSIDE.

HUH? WHY? WE'VE GOT LOTS OF TIME.

IT'S TOO SUNNY. MAYBE IF YOU DIDN'T PACK AWAY MY SUNGLASSES, WE COULD STILL SIT.

Late that night...

PLEASE REMAIN SEATED UNTIL OUR SICK PASSENGER HAS DE-PLANED...

GROAN

J.F.K.

SO THERE WAS A 6 HOUR DELAY BEFORE BOARDING. THEN VLADEK COMPLAINS THAT THE OXYGEN UNIT ISN'T WORKING AND HE CAN'T BREATHE.

THE CREW CHECKS AND SAYS THE UNIT IS FINE...

THEY SAY HE'S TOO SICK TO FLY, BUT WE REFUSE TO GET OFF. THEN VLADEK SAYS THE OXYGEN TANK *IS* WORKING, AND HERE WE ARE!

I'M GLAD YOU CALLED TO SAY YOU'D BE LATE.

THEY SET UP A FREE PHONE FOR DELAYED PASSENGERS. MALA CALLED EVERYONE SHE KNOWS IN AMERICA.

YOU SEE? I *LEARNED* FROM VLADEK!

A half hour later...

FINALLY! FRANÇOISE AND MALA MUST BE HOME AND DRY BY NOW. THEY COULD'VE DRIVEN US TO THE HOSPITAL.

DON'T WORRY, THE RIDE IS PAID BY MY *INSURANCE*.

EXCUSE ME. HE'S SICK, BUT I DON'T THINK HE NEEDS A STRETCHER.

REGULATIONS BUDDY.

SO, WHERE *IS* LAGUARDIA HOSPITAL?

ACH! GO ON QUEENS BOULEVARD 'TIL I SAY YOU TO TURN RIGHT.

THANKS, MISTER... BUT *PLEASE* STAY ON THE STRETCHER.

LaGuardia Hospital...

WE ARRIVED FINALLY TO HANNOVER...

THE KIDS CAN SHARE ONE BEDROOM. YOU TWO CAN HAVE THE OTHER...

DO YOU KNOW WHERE ANY OF **YOUR** FAMILY IS?

I'LL GO TO POLAND TO SEE IF ANYONE'S LEFT. WE PLANNED TO MEET IN SOSNOWIEC IF WE GOT SEPARATED.

I SENT A LETTER TO THE JEWISH COMMUNITY CENTER THERE, FOR MY WIFE, BUT— SHE CAN'T STILL BE ALIVE... I SAW HER IN AUSCHWITZ LAST YEAR...

SHE WAS SO THIN... SO WEAK...

YOU MIGHT GET NEWS ABOUT YOUR FAMILY AT THE BIG DP CAMP AT BELSEN. JEWS ARE FLOODING IN FROM ALL OVER.

IT WASN'T FAR, SO I WENT FOR A FEW DAYS TO BELSEN. ONE MORNING A CROWD ARRIVED IN, WITH TWO GIRLS WHAT I KNEW A LITTLE FROM MY HOME TOWN...

JENNY! SONIA!

LOOK! IT'S VLADEK SPIEGELMAN!

WE JUST CAME FROM POLAND...

WE WERE LUCKY TO GET OUT!...

WHATEVER YOU DO, DON'T GO BACK TO SOSNOWIEC. THE POLES ARE STILL KILLING JEWS THERE!

132

133

INCRED-IBLE!

YAH. SO, WHEN I HEARD ANJA IS *ALIVE* I STOPPED EVERYTHING TO GO ONLY BACK TO SOSNOWIEC.

I TRADED MY THINGS TO HAVE GIFTS.

LOOK! I GOT SOME DRESSES AND A FUR COAT TO BRING ANJA.

Y'KNOW, IF YOU GO TO POLAND, I'LL GO TOO!

WE WENT, SOMETIMES BY FOOT, SOMETIMES BY TRAIN.

TO POLAND, MANY TIMES IT WASN'T ANY *TRACKS* LEFT.

ONE PLACE WE STOPPED, HOURS, HOURS AND HOURS.

STAY HERE WITH OUR LUGGAGE, SHIVEK. I'LL GO FILL OUR CANTEENS.

I MARKED OUR TRAIN CAR, BUT WHEN I CAME IN AN HOUR BACK, IT WAS GONE TO ANOTHER TRACK

SHIVEK?!

I COULDN'T FIND MORE MY FRIEND AND MY LUGGAGE. I HAD ONLY MY THIN SHIRT AND MY WATER.

SHIVEK WENT BACK TO HAN-NOVER TO FIND ME AGAIN...

...BUT I WENT ONLY STRAIGHT TO POLAND. IT TOOK 3 OR 4 WEEKS.